7

SONGS ARE THOUGHTS
POEMS OF THE INUIT

Edited with an Introduction by Neil Philip

Illustrated by Maryclare Foa

DOUBLEDAY CANADA LIMITED

For Rachel and Emily
With love and gratitude to the Quinns and Eagle Island
In memory of J.H.C.
With best wishes and love to sweet Angus
— M.F.

Canadian Cataloguing in Publication Data

Main entry under title:

Songs are thoughts: poems of the Inuit

ISBN 0-385-25458-X

1. Inuit poetry – Translations into English
2. Children's poetry, Inuit – Translations into English. I. Foa, Maryclare, 1956-

PM50.295E6 1995   897.1   C93-095518-8

2 3 4 5 6 7 8 9 10

Jacket design by Alan Peacock
Typesetting by York House Typographic
Color origination by York House Graphics
Printed and bound in Italy

An Albion Book
Conceived, designed and produced by The Albion Press Ltd
Spring Hill, Idbury, Oxfordshire OX7 6RU
Designer: Emma Bradford
Project Manager: Elizabeth Wilkes

First published 1995 by
Doubleday Canada Limited
105 Bond Street
Toronto, Ontario
M 5B 1Y3

Introduction

The poems in this book were not written to be read, but composed to be sung. The making of such songs is an important element of traditional Inuit life in Greenland, northern Canada, and Alaska — everyone makes songs just as everyone breathes. Indeed, the Inuit word *anerca* signifies both "breath" and "poetry." The poet Orpingalik said, "All my being is song, and I sing as I draw breath."

The songs, composed in the long Arctic hours of solitude and stillness, reflect every aspect of Inuit life. Many are about hunting, fishing, canoeing, berry gathering, but others are about personal feelings, and still others explore the great mysteries of life and death. They are meant to be shared — sung or chanted at gatherings at which, recalled the Danish/Inuit explorer, Knud Rasmussen, "words, music, and dance mingled into one great wave of feeling." He writes:

> The singer stands in the middle of the floor, with
> knees slightly bent, the upper part of the body
> bowed slightly forward, swaying from the hips, and
> rising and sinking from the knees with a rhythmic
> movement, keeping time throughout with his own
> beating of the drum. Then he begins to sing, keeping
> his eyes shut all the time; for a singer and a poet
> must always look inward in thought, concentrating
> on his own emotion.

Poets such as Orpingalik composed many songs; he described them as his "comrades in solitude." But the private satisfaction of finding the right words, the right tune, to express what needed to be said, was only half of the creative process; public performance was the other half. This becomes clear in the biting, sarcastic "Song to a Miser" collected by Rasmussen in East Greenland.

> I put some words together,
> I made a little song,
> I took it home one evening,
> Mysteriously wrapped, disguised.
> Underneath my bed it went:
> Nobody was going to share it,
> Nobody was going to taste it!
> I wanted it for me! me! me!
> Secret, undivided!

This mingling of the private thought and the public act is so complete that both lighthearted quarrels and deep personal grievances can be sorted out by a kind of song duel, in which the opposing poets hurl finely turned insults at each other.

The Inuit live in a harsh, unforgiving environment. There is a stripped-to-the-bone quality about their songs that echoes this. But there is also a sense of openness to what lies beyond the elemental world. One man, Satdlagé, told the following story to explain why he no longer joined in at song festivals.

Once, when I was quite a young man, I wanted to
compose a song about my village, and for a whole
winter evening I walked up and down in the
moonlight, trying to fit words together that
would go with a tune I was humming. I did find the
words: excellent words that would convey to my
friends the beauty of the mountains and every
delightful thing I saw when I went outside and
opened my eyes. Pacing up and down on the frozen
snow, I became so preoccupied with my thoughts
that I quite forgot where I was. Suddenly I stop and
lift my head. And look! In front of me, the mountain
near our village rises higher and steeper than I
have ever seen it. It was almost as if it was very
slowly growing out of the earth and coming to lean
over me, dangerous and threatening. It was then
that I heard a voice coming from the air. "Little
man!" it cried. "The echo of your words has reached
me! Do you really think I can be contained in your
song?"

This sense of living in a world that has a spiritual reality, as well as a physical one, is very
strong in many Inuit poems, particularly those by poets such as Orpingalik, Aua, Igjugarjuk, and
Uvavnuk, who were *angákoqs*, or shamans — spiritual leaders and healers.

Native American oral poets have often been described as "singing for power," and this
phrase expresses something true about the work of the poets in this book. Orpingalik, a
shaman of the Netsilik people of Hudson Bay, opens his poem "My Breath" with the words,

I will sing a song,
A song that is strong.

The "strength" of such a song — which might contain special "magic" words that were not
meant to be understood — rested, in the end, in the shared belief of all poets that language
itself is a kind of magic. As Rasmussen puts it, discussing the poems of Aua's brother
Ivaluardjuk, "No one can become a poet who has not complete faith in the power of words."
Such words might be simple, as in the case of Aua's spontaneous song when, in "a fit of
mysterious and overwhelming delight," he became a shaman.

I felt a great inexplicable joy, a joy so powerful
that I could not restrain it, but had to break into
song, a mighty song, with only room for the one
word: joy, joy!

These poems are full of such joy, a joy that mixes fear and wonder with delight in simply
being alive. For the Inuit, wrote Diamond Jenness, "songs are constantly interspersed with cries
and laughter."

Living always on the edge of hardship — even starvation — these poets choose to
celebrate, not bemoan, their lot. In the words of Qúpaq, "Luck nearly always follows after
misfortune. If this were not so, people would soon die out."

— *Neil Philip*

Songs are Thoughts

Songs are thoughts, sung out with the breath when people are moved by great forces and ordinary speech no longer suffices.

Man is moved just like the ice floe sailing here and there out in the current. His thoughts are driven by a flowing force when he feels joy, when he feels fear, when he feels sorrow. Thoughts can wash over him like a flood, making his breath come in gasps and his heart throb. Something like an abatement in the weather will keep him thawed up. And then it will happen that we, who always think we are small, will feel still smaller. And we will fear to use words. When the words we want to use shoot up of themselves — we get a new song.

Orpingalik

MORNING PRAYER

I rise up from rest,
Moving swiftly as the raven's wing
I rise up to meet the day —
Wa-wa.

My face is turned from the dark of night
My gaze towards the dawn,
Toward the whitening dawn.

Aua

THE JOY OF A SINGER

A wonderful occupation
Making songs!
But all too often they
Are failures.

A wonderful fate
Getting wishes fulfilled!
But all too often they
Slip past.

A wonderful occupation
Hunting caribou!
But all too rarely we
Excel at it
So that we stand
Like a bright flame
Over the plain.

Piuvkaq

THE MOTHER'S SONG

It is so still in the house,
There is a calm in the house;
The snowstorm wails out there,
And the dogs are rolled up with snouts under the tail.
My little boy is sleeping on the ledge,
On his back he lies, breathing through his open mouth.
His little stomach is bulging round —
Is it strange if I start to cry with joy?

Anonymous

MUSK OXEN

Yai-yai-yai
Ya-ayai-ya
I ran with all speed
And met them on the plain,
The great musk ox with brilliant black hair —
Hayai-ya-haya.

It was the first time I had seen them,
Grazing on the flowers of the plain,
Far from the hill where I stood,
And ignorantly I thought
They were but small and slight . . .

But they grew up out of the earth
As I came within shot,
Great black giant beasts
Far from our dwellings
In the regions of happy summer hunting.

Igjugarjuk

PERSONAL SONG

It is a time of hunger,
But I don't feel like hunting,
I don't care for the advice of the old people,
I only care for dreaming, wishing, nothing else.
I only care for gossip;
I am fond of young caribou, the age they start getting their antlers;
Nobody is like me,
I am too lazy, simply too lazy,
I just can't bring myself to go and get some meat.

Arnatkoak

THE GULL

The gull, it is said,
The one who cleaves the air with its wings
The one that is usually above you
Gull, you up there
Steer down towards me
Come to me
Your wings
Are red
Up there — in the coolness.

Nakasuk

BEAR HUNTING

I spied a bear
On the drifting floe
Like a harmless dog
It came running and wagging its tail towards me
But all so eager to eat me up
That it swung round snarling
When I leaped aside.
And now came a game of catch-me-who-can
That lasted from morning till late in the day.
But at last it was wearied
And could play no more,
So I thrust my spear into its side.

Aua

SONG OF JOY

The great sea
Has set me adrift,
It moves me as the weed in a great river,
Earth and the great weather
Move me,
Have carried me away
And move my inward parts with joy.

Uvavnuk

WORDS

Amaija-ai, ja-jai, ai-ja,
I'm a timid man —
A quietly spoken one —
Never mocking,
Never heaping evil words
On men.
That's my way,
That's how I am,
Amaja-ja.
Words cause movement,
Words bring calm,
Words tell the truth,
And words tell lies,
Amaja-ja-ja!

Anonymous (Umanatsiaq)

THE OLD MAN'S SONG

I have grown old,
I have lived much,
Many things I understand,
But four riddles I cannot solve.
Ha-ya-ya-ya.

The sun's origin,
The moon's nature,
The minds of women,
And why people have so many lice.
Ha-ya-ya-ya.

Anonymous